OGG AND BOB

Meet Mammoth

By
Ian Fraser

Illustrated by
Mary Ann Fraser

To Ann and her students,

two lions

M Fraser

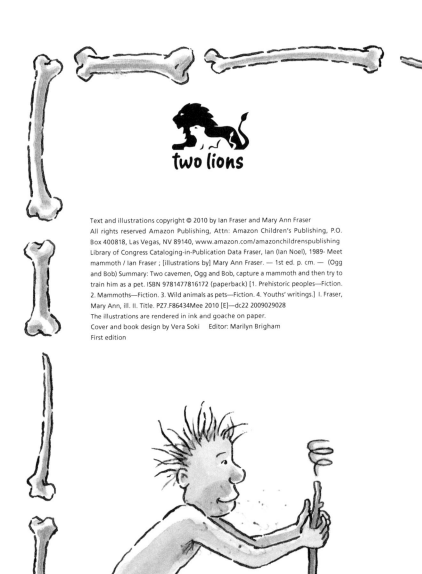

two lions

Text and illustrations copyright © 2010 by Ian Fraser and Mary Ann Fraser
All rights reserved Amazon Publishing, Attn: Amazon Children's Publishing, P.O.
Box 400818, Las Vegas, NV 89140, www.amazon.com/amazonchildrenspublishing
Library of Congress Cataloging-in-Publication Data Fraser, Ian (Ian Noel), 1989- Meet
mammoth / Ian Fraser ; [illustrations by] Mary Ann Fraser. — 1st ed. p. cm. — (Ogg
and Bob) Summary: Two cavemen, Ogg and Bob, capture a mammoth and then try to
train him as a pet. ISBN 9781477816172 (paperback) [1. Prehistoric peoples—Fiction.
2. Mammoths—Fiction. 3. Wild animals as pets—Fiction. 4. Youths' writings.] I. Fraser,
Mary Ann, ill. II. Title. PZ7.F86434Mee 2010 [E]—dc22 2009029028
The illustrations are rendered in ink and goache on paper.
Cover and book design by Vera Soki   Editor: Marilyn Brigham
First edition

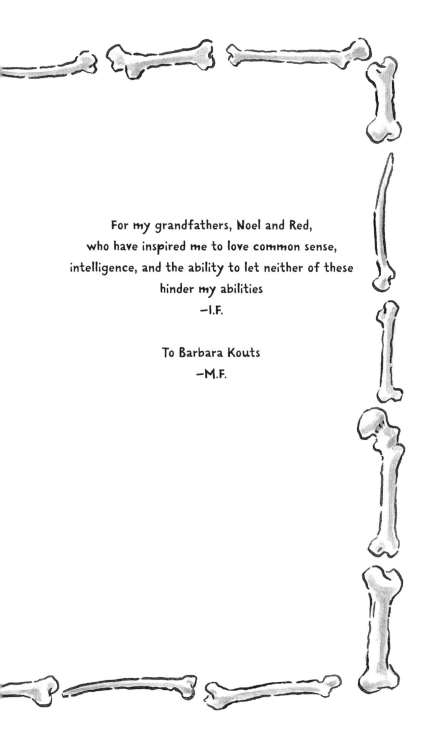

For my grandfathers, Noel and Red,
who have inspired me to love common sense,
intelligence, and the ability to let neither of these
hinder my abilities
—I.F.

To Barbara Kouts
—M.F.

Contents

Meet the Characters

This is Ogg. He lives in a cave with his best friend, Bob, and his pet mammoth, Mug. Ogg is good at thinking of things to do. Ogg doesn't like baths. He likes rocks and food, but most of all he loves to play with Bob and Mug.

This is Bob. Bob lives in a cave with his best friend, Ogg, and his pet mammoth, Mug. He is good at solving the problems that he and Ogg encounter. Bob doesn't like bugs or being eaten by saber-tooth tigers. He likes thinking and exploring with Ogg and Mug.

This is Mug. Mug is Ogg and Bob's large, hairy pet mammoth. He is good at causing problems. Mug likes to eat, sleep, and play games.

This is Saber-tooth Tiger. He is good at hunting. Saber-tooth Tiger likes to eat mammoths and cavemen with his two big teeth. This is a problem for Ogg, Bob, and Mug.

Chapter 1
A New Pet

One day, Ogg and Bob went for a walk.

"Look!" said Ogg. "There's mammoth! Mammoth make good pet."

"Mammoth too big," said Bob.

"Not too big," said Ogg.

"Too big," said Bob.

"Not too big," said Ogg.

Bob was tired of arguing. "Okay," he said.

"How catch mammoth?" asked Bob.

"Hit with rock!" said Ogg.

"No," said Bob. "We catch in pit!"

"Rock!" yelled Ogg.

"Pit!" yelled Bob.

"Rock!" yelled Ogg.

"Pit!" yelled Bob.

Ogg was tired of arguing. "Okay," he said.

The two friends found a deep hole.

"Cover hole with sticks," said Bob.

"Cover hole with grass," said Ogg.

"Sticks," said Bob.

"Grass," said Ogg.

They were both tired of arguing, so they used grass *and* sticks.

But then . . . SNAP!

"Uh-oh," said Ogg.

Down they fell into the pit.

"Think of way out," said Bob.

"Head hurt," said Ogg.

"From fall?" asked Bob.

"From thinking," said Ogg.

"Stop snorting in ear," Bob said.
"Not me," said Ogg.
"Then who?" asked Bob.

"MAMMOTH!" cried Ogg. He grabbed the mammoth's trunk. "ME CATCH MAMMOTH!"

The mammoth flung Ogg into a nearby tree.

"Wheeeeeeeeeeeeeeeee!" yelled Ogg.

"Me catch mammoth, too," said Bob. He grabbed the mammoth's trunk.

The mammoth flung Bob into the tree.

"Wheeeeeeeeeeeeeeeee!" yelled Bob.

Now both friends were stuck in the tree.

"Me climb down," said Bob.

"Not good idea," said Ogg. "SEE TIGER!"
"ROAR!"

Bob scrambled back up the tree. "Big kitty,"
he said.

"Na-na-na-na-na-na!" teased Ogg, as he shook a stick at the tiger.

The tiger snarled and caught hold of the end of the stick. "Help!" yelled Ogg.

The tree started to bend. And bend. And bend.

"Me help!" said Bob. He leaned way over and smacked the tiger's paw.

"Wheeeeeeeeeeeeeee

!" 	The tiger let go. The tree shot Ogg and Bob into the air.

They landed on the mammoth's soft head.

"Thanks, Mammoth," said Ogg.

"Mammoth make good pet," said Bob.

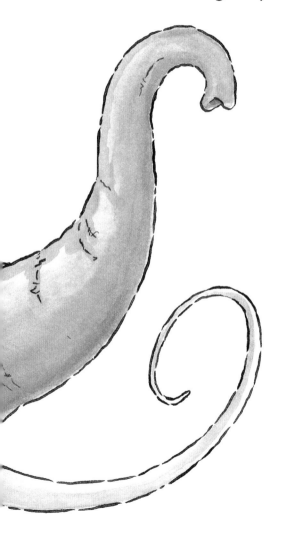

"Me name him Bob!" said Ogg.
"Bob my name!" complained Bob.
"Okay," said Ogg. "How about Mug?"
"Mug good name," Bob agreed.
They took Mug to his new home.

Chapter 2

Mammoth Training

Ogg and Bob were busy eating lunch.

Mug wanted Ogg and Bob to play with him. He trampled their beds. He ran through the fire pit. He scattered food everywhere.

"What a mess!" shouted Bob. "Mug need to play outside."

"Mug, OUT!" shouted Ogg.

Mug continued to bounce around the cave.

"Mug not listen," said Bob. "Maybe mammoth bad pet after all."

"Mug good pet! You see! Mug just need training," replied Ogg.

"How we train Mug?" asked Bob.

"Show Mug what OUT means," suggested Ogg. "Help push Mug out."

"Okay," said Bob.

Ogg and Bob got behind Mug and pushed. "Mug, OUT," they said together.

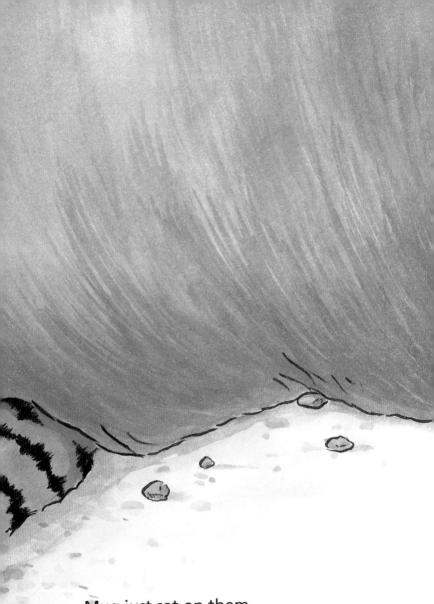

Mug just sat on them.

"Oww!" they cried. "We say OUT, not SIT!" shouted Ogg and Bob.

Ogg grabbed Mug's tail and pulled. Mug jumped up. He ran outside. Ogg and Bob followed him.

"OUT not work very well. Maybe try COME," said Bob, after Mug let them down.

"Good idea," said Ogg.

"COME, Mug!" they both shouted.

Mug did not listen. He ran around chasing his tail.

"Mug not COME," said Ogg.

"Maybe Mug not hear us," said Bob. "Let's get closer."

Ogg and Bob ran toward Mug. "COME, MUG!" they shouted.

Mug thought it was a game. He ran off.

"Mug confused," said Bob.

"He thinks we mean GO," said Ogg.

They chased Mug up the hill and through the creek. They chased him around the trees and all the way back to the cave.

They were all out of breath.

"Chased Mug everywhere, and Mug still not learn COME," complained Bob.

Ogg sighed. "Maybe mammoth *is* bad pet."

"Wait! I have idea," said Bob.

"Mug, STAY!" Bob yelled.

Mug was too tired to move.

"We did it!" they cheered. "We train Mug! He STAY!"

"Mug *is* good pet," said Bob.

Mug waved his trunk at Ogg and Bob.

Mug rolled over.
"What Mug doing?" asked Ogg.
"Mug want belly scratch," said Bob.

They scratched Mug's tummy.

"Hey! We not train Mug. Mug train us!" said Ogg and Bob.

Snort-snoorkle-snuff!

Chapter 3
Getting Some Sleep

Ogg and Bob had a long, tiring day. Taking care of Mug was hard work.

They couldn't wait to go to bed. But as they lay down to get some sleep, a sound cut through the silence of the cave. *Snort-snoorkle-snuff!*

"What that?" grumbled Ogg.

"It Mug," mumbled Bob.

"Mug loud," said Ogg. "Give me headache." He moaned.

"Wake Mug up with tickles!" suggested Bob.

Ogg tickled Mug's feet. Bob tickled Mug behind the ears.

Mug thrashed around in his sleep. The cave started to shake. Rocks fell, but Mug did not wake up.

"Maybe better to let sleeping mammoth snore," suggested Bob.

"No, me make mammoth quiet," said Ogg.

"How?" asked Bob.

"With rock!" said Ogg. Ogg grabbed a large rock in the cave. He plugged Mug's trunk with it.

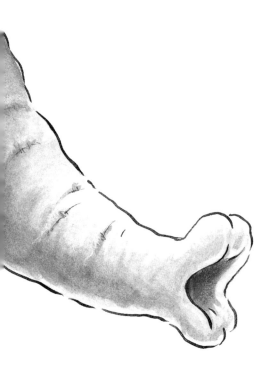

All of a sudden: *SNUFF-SNUFF-SNORT—WHAM!*

Mug shot the rock out of his trunk.

The rock hit Ogg in the head.

"You okay?" asked Bob.

"Me have bigger headache now," said Ogg.

"I have best idea yet," said Bob. "We plug ears with grass."

"Why plug Mug ears?" asked Ogg.

"Not mammoth's ears," said Bob. "*Our* ears."

"Oh," said Ogg.

"Why ears itch?" asked Ogg.
"What?" Bob took out the grass.
"Why ears itch?" asked Ogg again.
"BUGS!" yelled Bob.

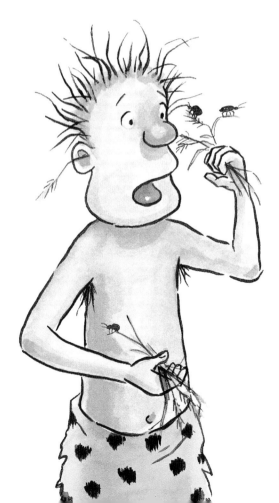

Ogg and Bob dashed outside. They rolled around in the mud. They splashed around in the river until all the bugs were off.

"Me tired," said Ogg, when they were back in the cave.

"Me, too," said Bob.

Ogg and Bob drifted off to sleep.

But all of a sudden . . .

. . . snort-snoorkle-snuff!

Mug went outside to sleep, away from all the snoring.

As a child, **Ian Fraser** loved playing "caveman," and he is still intrigued by cavemen to this day. *Ogg and Bob* is exactly the type of book he would have wanted to read as a kid. These days, Ian is attending college and dreaming up even more stories about Ogg and Bob. He lives in San Luis Obispo, California.

Mary Ann Fraser is the author and illustrator of many books for children, including *Mermaid Sister*, *Pet Shop Lullaby*, and the I.Q. series. Her awards include *School Library Journal* Book of the Year, an International Reading Association Young Readers' Choice Award, and a *Book Sense* Children's Pick. She lives and paints in a cave in Simi Valley, California. Visit her Web site to learn more: www.MaryAnnFraser.com

Made in the USA
Charleston, SC
29 September 2013